Favorite Fairy Tales

Snow White and Rose Red

Favorite Fairy Tales

Compiled by Cooper Edens and Harold Darling of
The Blue Lantern Studio

CHRONICLE BOOKS • SAN FRANCISCO

Cover Design: Brenda Rae Eno

Printed in Hong Kong

Library of Congress Cataloging-in-Publication Data

A Classic illustrated edition : favorite fairytales.
p.   cm.
Summary: A collection of fourteen classic fairy tales, including "Hansel and Gretel," "Snow White," and "Puss in Boots," featuring antique illustrations.
ISBN 0-87701-848-0
1. Fairy tales. [1. Fairy tales. 2. Folklore] I. Chronicle Books (Firm) II. Title: Favorite fairytales.
PZ8.C57   1991
398.21—dc20
90-22607
CIP
AC

Distributed in Canada by Raincoast Books,
112 East Third Avenue, Vancouver, B.C. V5T 1C8

2   4   6   8   10   9   7   5   3   1

Chronicle Books
275 Fifth Street
San Francisco, California 94103

Table Of Contents

Preface

Fairy tales are stories set in magical, timeless realms where the rules and logic of our ordinary world do not apply. Animals talk, objects (like beanstalks and broomsticks) take on lives of their own, giants and ogres appear out of nowhere, curses and magic spells create havoc, witches and wizards have wondrous powers, and, of course, fairies and elves abound. These are stories that address very basic and universal human emotions, and the simplicity of their morals or messages often belies their important psychological depth.

Because fairy stories often emerge from folklore—from stories that have been told again and again beside campfires and before hearths—they have a universality that goes beyond the individual story, and frequently similar stories can be found in a variety of cultures. At some point, an author decides to write the story down and, in the writing, usually gives it some sort of literary shaping. It is this literary tradition that often separates fairy tales from their folk counterparts. The Grimm Brothers and Charles Perrault are the most important of these collectors and the majority of the stories in this volume are from their books.

There is always a process of selection in the world's endless sorting of stories. Those which storytellers remember are those that they like the best and which their audiences respond to most favorably.

From their repertoires, just a few live to be told by following generations. Only those stories that can transcend the changes of fashion and interest or the barriers of language and geography can survive the passage of time. It is through this process that the vast ocean of stories is winnowed down to a small, sparkling lake-sized group of select tales.

Out of this small group, we have chosen what we believe to be the cream of the fairy stories. We have paired each story with illustrations from antique sources, choosing in each case the one artist who seemed in deepest sympathy with that particular tale. Thus, what we have gathered together is our favorite fairy tales illustrated with our favorite pictures. We hope there will be much in it for you to remember.

The Sleeping Beauty

IN a place and time long past, there lived a King and Queen who had a lovely baby girl. When the baby was born, the King decreed that there would be a celebration, and to the great feast he invited the twelve fairy godmothers of his kingdom.

Now some of the more ancient subjects remarked that in their day, there had been thirteen fairy godmothers, but few had heard of the thirteenth in many years. Besides, the King reasoned, he had only twelve golden plates and twelve golden goblets, so it seemed to make sense that only twelve fairy godmothers be invited.

The day of the celebration came at last and the fairy god-mothers arrived at the palace. They gathered round the cradle of the baby Princess and promised her all sorts of delightful things: that she should be the most beautiful in the whole world; that she should be the sweetest-tempered; that she should be the cleverest; that she should sing like a lark; that she should dance like a blos-som on the wind; that everyone should love her; and that she should never lack gold. The King and Queen were delighted.

Suddenly, the Lord High Chamberlain came running with a very white face to announce that yet *another* fairy guest had arrived. The King and Queen hastened to welcome this unex-pected fairy. They led her to a chair at the head of the table and begged her to honor them by partaking of the good things spread forth there.

The thirteenth fairy was exceedingly annoyed.

"You had forgotten me," she said, "but I shall give you good cause to remember me hereafter. My sisters have promised many fair gifts to your daughter. My promise is that she shall prick her finger on a spindle and die!"

At these cruel words everyone uttered a loud cry. The Queen burst into tears. The King tore at his beard. The Lord High Chamberlain sobbed aloud. Then the youngest of the fairy god-mothers stepped forward and said, "Be comforted, good people. Though I have not the power to undo what my sister has done, I can alter the spell this much—that the Princess shall *not* die of the prick."

At these words, the Queen wiped her eyes, the King ceased to tear his beard, and the Lord High Chamberlain stopped short in the middle of a sob.

"Wait," said the fairy, "I have not finished yet. When the Princess pricks her finger she shall fall asleep, and she shall not wake again till the most gallant Prince finds her and kisses her on the cheek."

When the fairies had departed, the first thing that the King did was to set forth a new law. From that day on, no one should spin in his dominions, and all spinning wheels and spindles were to be either burned or thrown into the sea. Sixteen years passed, without the hum of a single spinning wheel. The Princess grew up beautiful, clever, and good, just as her godmothers had promised.

One fine day, when her father was out hunting and her mother and all the maids of honor were gathering cherries, the Princess decided to explore some of the ancient parts of the palace. She went from room to room, and from tower to tower, climbing up narrow, twisting staircases. At last she came to a little door at the very top of a high tower. From behind the door came a low humming sound such as she had never heard before.

Full of curiosity, the Princess opened the door and found an aged woman working with a wheel. Nobody had thought of telling this old woman about the law forbidding people to spin, and for sixteen years hers had been the only spinning wheel in the land.

"What are you doing, good woman?" asked the Princess.

"I am spinning, my pretty young lady."

"Is it very difficult to spin?"

"Not for one who has clear eyes and willing fingers."

"Will you not show me how it is done?"

"Gladly, my pretty one. 'Tis many a long year now since I saw a young face in this old tower."

The Princess sat down beside the aged woman, eager to learn. But in her eagerness, she seized the spindle by the sharp end and the point pricked her finger. Only one tiny drop of blood appeared, but the poor Princess slipped from her chair as if she were dead.

In great terror, the woman ran to fetch help. When the Princess had been carried down the twisting stairs and laid upon her own golden bed, the King and Queen saw the drop of blood on her finger and knew that the cruel fairy's promise had been fulfilled.

Wild with sorrow, they ran out of the palace and hurried toward the castle where the youngest fairy dwelt.

"You need not tell me why you are so sad," the fairy said, "for I know what has happened. You will never see your child again. Nor can you return to your palace, for my cruel sister has already surrounded it by a thick tangle of briars."

"Oh, kind fairy," cried the King and Queen, "can you do nothing to help us?"

"I have done all that I can. When your daughter wakes, she will find her maids of honor and her pages and even her pets near her, for they have fallen into the same enchanted sleep as she, and when she opens her eyes they will open *theirs*."

With this promise the poor King and Queen had to be content. As the sleeping Princess was their only child, the crown passed to a distant branch of the family after the King and Queen's death. By degrees, people began to forget what had happened and to say that the story of the enchanted sleep was only an old fairy-tale.

A hundred years passed and nobody tried to enter the thorn forest until one fine morning, the son of the present King was out hunting and galloped so far that he found himself in a lonely valley on the edge of a gloomy wood. No one was in sight, except an old woodcutter.

"I am sure I do not know this place," thought the Prince, "I must certainly have lost my way. I wonder if there is a castle anywhere about."

He beckoned to the woodcutter and said, "Good fellow, it seems to me that I have lost my way. Is there a castle anywhere near here, where a hungry sportsman would be kindly received?"

The old man shook his head. "There be no castles hereabouts, young sir, nor no houses either. 'Tis as lonesome a piece o' country as any in the kingdom. My father *did* say there was a castle yonder, in that wood, and a sleeping Princess in it, too. But I don't heed those old tales."

In his childhood the Prince had heard the story of the Sleeping Beauty, but he had forgotten all about it until this moment. As he was a brave and gallant youth, he determined to try to force his way through the tangled branches to find out for himself if there really was a Sleeping Beauty. The Prince tied his horse to a tree and offered the woodcutter a piece of gold in exchange for his axe. The offer was quickly accepted, but the Prince soon found that he did not need the axe. The moment he touched the branches with his hand, they came unknotted and sprang apart.

Deeper and deeper into the briar of thorns the Prince made his way. After he had walked about a mile, he reached the great and stately palace. The door stood open and so he walked boldly in. Everything was silent inside the palace.

On tiptoe he passed from one beautiful room to another, some with walls of looking-glass, some with walls of mother-of-pearl, some with walls of ivory. At last, in the very center of the palace, he came to the room where the Princess lay in her enchanted sleep. At either end of her golden bed sat a lady-in-waiting, as fast asleep as she. Across the threshold her page slept, with his lute in his hand. At her feet slumbered a fluffy white dog, and in the silver cage by her pillow three little birds with brightly colored plumes were dreaming, each with his head tucked under his wing.

If the Prince had paused to look at the ladies and at the page, he would have recognized their dress as being the costume worn by the people of that land more than a hundred years before. But he could not look at anyone or at anything, except the Princess. Her hair had grown and grown, till it covered her from head to foot with a mantle more lovely than the richest cloth of gold.

Of course, being a Prince and having heard the story of the Sleeping Beauty in his childhood, he knew exactly what to do. He bent forward and kissed her. Immediately the three little birds began to sing, and the little white dog began to bark, the ladies-in-waiting rubbed their eyes, the page sat up and went on with his playing. Then the Princess opened her eyes and held out her hand to the Prince, saying joyfully, "Oh, I have been waiting *such* a long time for you to come and wake me!"

As for the rest of this story, that you'll have to guess for yourself.

The original version of this story was first published in 1696. The illustrations are by Arthur Rackham and were first published in 1920.

Rumpelstiltskin

THERE once was a poor miller who had a beautiful daughter. One day, the miller had an audience with the King and in order to make himself seem more important, he told the King that his daughter could spin straw into gold. The King was very fond of gold and thought to himself, "This is an art which would please me very much." So he said to the miller, "If your daughter is so very clever, bring her to the castle in the morning and I will put her to the test."

As soon as the miller's daughter arrived, the King led her into a chamber filled with straw. He gave her a spinning wheel and said, "If you have not spun this straw into gold by tomorrow morning, your father will be killed."

There she sat for a very long time, thinking how to save her father's life. Since she had never heard of straw being turned into gold, she could think of nothing, and so at last she began to weep.

All at once, the door opened and in stepped an odd little man who said, "Good evening, fair maiden. Why do you weep?"

"Ah," she replied, "I must spin this straw into gold, and I am sure I do not know how."

"What will you give me if I spin it for you?" the little man asked.

"My necklace," answered the maiden.

The little man took the necklace, placed himself in front of the spinning wheel, and whirr, whirr, whirr three times round and the bobbin was full. Then he set up another, and whirr, whirr,

whirr, thrice round again, and a second bobbin was full. And so he went all night long, until all the straw was gone and all the bobbins were full of gold.

At sunrise, the King came to the chamber and was astonished to see the gold. Then he led the maiden into a larger room filled with straw and bade her spin it into gold during the night if she valued her father's life. The maiden was again at a loss. But while she cried, the door opened and once again the little man appeared and asked what she would give him in return for his assistance.

"My ring," she replied.

The little man took the ring and began to spin. By morning all the straw was changed into glistening gold. The King rejoiced at the sight, but still he was not satisfied. He led the maiden into yet a larger chamber full of straw and said, "This you must spin during the night. If you accomplish it, you shall be my bride."

When the maiden was left alone, the little man appeared and asked for the third time, "What will you give me to do this for you?"

"I have nothing left," replied the maiden.

"Then promise me that if you become Queen, you will give me your first-born child," said the little man.

Rumpelstiltskin

The miller's daughter thought to herself, "Who can tell if that will ever happen?" Having no other way to help herself out of her trouble, she promised him what he wished. The little man immediately set to spinning. Whirr, whirr, whirr he went all through the night and when morning came, the King found all he had wished for. So they had a great wedding feast and the miller's daughter became Queen.

A year or so later, when the Queen had forgotten all about the little man, she brought a fine child into the world. But the little man had not forgotten her promise, and he soon appeared and demanded she fulfill that promise. The frightened Queen offered him all the riches of the kingdom if he would leave the child, but the little man answered, "No, something human is dearer to me than all the wealth of the world."

The Queen began to weep so much that the little man felt sorry for her and said, "I will give you three days to think. If you can guess my name in that time, you shall keep the child."

A messenger was sent far and wide through the kingdom to collect new names and all night long the Queen racked her brains to think of a name. The following day, the little man returned. The Queen began with "Caspar," "Melchior," "Balthasar," and all the odd names she knew. But with each guess, the little man exclaimed, "That is not my name!"

The second day, the Queen asked all her people for curious and uncommon names. "Ribs-of-Beef," "Sheepshank," "Whale-bone," but at each the little man said, "That is not my name!"

On the third day, the messenger returned and said, "I have not found a single name, but as I came to a high mountain at the edge of the forest, I saw a little house. Before the door a fire was burning and round this fire a curious little man was bouncing on one leg and shouting:

"Today I stew and later I'll bake,
Tomorrow the Queen's child I'll take.
Worthless is her fortune and fame,
For nobody knows Rumpelstiltskin's my name!"

When the Queen heard this, she was delighted. Soon afterward, the little man arrived and asked, "Now my Lady Queen, what is my name?"

First, she said, "Are you called Conrad?"

"No."

"Are you called Hal?"

"No."

Rumpelstiltskin

"Are you called Rumpelstiltskin?"

"A witch has told you! A witch has told you!" shrieked the little man, and he stamped and stamped his foot so hard that it went right through the floor and he could not get it out again. So he hopped away on one foot, howling terribly, and the Queen has not heard from her troublesome visitor since.

The original version of this story was first published in 1882. The illustrations are by George R. Halkett and were first published in 1882.

Puss in Boots

IN a red-roofed windmill on top of a hill, there once lived a miller and his three sons. When the miller died, he left his property to be divided among the three. To the eldest he left his red-roofed windmill. To the second, he left his gray donkey. And to the third he left his golden cat.

The eldest son soon got the mill turning and the second son decided to stay on so that his donkey could carry the sacks to market. But there was no place for the youngest, so he bade his brothers farewell and set off to seek his fortune, his faithful cat at his side.

After they had walked for several miles, the young man sat down to rest. As he sat there, he suddenly thought what a comical thing it was that his only legacy was a golden-colored Puss sitting at his feet. He burst out laughing, exclaiming, "It is really a very good joke."

"Better than you know!" said a small voice.

The young man looked to the left, he looked to the right, he looked behind him, and he looked up in the air, but there was nobody to be seen. Then he looked *down*, and the same voice said, "You didn't know I could talk, did you?"

"Well," he said when he had recovered from his astonishment, "I am very glad that you can talk, for you are the only friend I have. If you stick with me, I am not likely to feel lonely or sad."

"I am quite willing to stick with you," returned the cat, "But I find walking on the road very hard work. You have a pair of spare boots in your bag. Why not lend them to me?"

"You'd be welcome to my boots," laughed the boy, "but they are far too large."

"Let's see," urged the cat. So his master untied his bundle and gave the cat the boots. Each boot seemed large enough to hold the cat's whole body. Yet when he started to pull them on, they shrank in size until they were an excellent fit.

"That's a good joke!" cried the young man.

"Better than you know," returned the cat, strutting about proudly in his boots. "Now I have another favor to ask. I want you to throw your bundle into the river and let me have the handkerchief in which it was tied up."

"But, my good Puss," said the young man, "this bundle contains everything in the world that I possess."

"And that's not much," said the cat. "Still, if you will do as I ask, I promise that you will gain much more than you will lose."

The young man was beginning to see that this cat was no ordinary cat, so his poor bundle was dropped into the river.

"Now, master," said the cat, "Wait here till I return. I shall not come back with empty paws, I promise you."

The young man promised to wait, as the cat ran off into the woods with the handkerchief over his shoulder. When Puss was deep in the woods, he knotted the handkerchief into a bag and put some sweet clover inside it. Then he lay down and pretended to be asleep. A little rabbit soon came and nibbled at the clover.

"Go away!" said the cat, opening one bright green eye.

Soon, a larger rabbit appeared and began to nibble the clover.

"Go away," said the cat, opening the other bright green eye.

Finally, a big, fat rabbit arrived. No sooner had he begun to nibble than Puss jumped up and pulled the bag over the rabbit's head. Then he slung the bag across his shoulder and ran and ran till he came to a castle, which stood at the end of the woods.

The King was just going out when Puss came running up and laid the handsome rabbit respectfully before the royal feet.

"What is this?" asked the King.

"Sir, it is a rabbit from the famous warren of my master, the Marquis of Carabas, which he begs you to accept."

"I am much obliged to the Marquis," said the King. "I never saw a finer rabbit in my life. Take this piece of gold, Mr. Puss in Boots, as a token of my favor."

The cat thanked the King with a low bow and then ran back to his master as fast as he could. "Master," said the cat, "here is a piece of gold. And I have something else to give you."

"What's that Puss?" asked the astonished youth.

"A new name. Henceforth you are to be the Marquis of Carabas."

At this, the young man burst out laughing. "As you please, Puss. But it seems a good joke to me."

"Better than you know," said the cat.

The next day, the cat caught two plump partridges and offered them to the King from the Marquis of Carabas.

"The Marquis is very kind," said the King. "Where *are* these estates upon which such splendid game is to be found."

"Does your Majesty not know?" asked the cat. "Why, the finest forests and fairest meadows are all his."

"I am greatly interested to hear it," said the King as he gave the cat two pieces of gold.

The next day, Puss in Boots told the miller's son that he must go and bathe in the river at an hour when the royal party would be riding along the bank. "Remember," added the cat, "that if anyone tries to pull you out of the water, you must let them."

"That sounds like a good joke," said the boy.

"Better than you know," returned the cat.

No sooner had the Marquis of Carabas plunged into the river, than Puss in Boots ran toward the royal party and mewed at the top of of voice, "Help, help, my noble master, the Marquis of Carabas, is drowning!"

"Two of my guards will save him," said the King. The two guards lept from their horses, dove into the river, and brought the astonished boy ashore.

"I should be glad to meet this Marquis of Carabas," said the King.

"Alas, Sire, answered the cat, "while the noble Marquis was bathing, some thief stole his silk garments and left these poor rags in their place. He cannot appear before your Majesty and your daughter, Her Royal Highness, in such a plight."

"We can soon put that right," said the King. "There is a spare suit of clothes in that hamper. Take it to the Marquis with my good wishes."

When the miller's son approached the royal party in his new clothes, both the King and the Princess were much struck by the handsome looks and the good-natured manner of the Marquis of Carabas.

"You have wide lands and rich forests, Marquis," remarked the King. "How many acres do your estates cover in all?"

"I should have great difficulty in telling your Majesty," replied the Marquis.

"He must be very rich," thought the King, so he invited his new acquaintance to ride a little way with him.

The Marquis rode between the King and Princess, while the cat kept pace alongside.

"Master," said the cat, speaking loudly enough that the King could hear, "we are now drawing near your estates. I will run ahead and prepare the way."

"We cannot go too far," remarked the King, "for beyond that mountain there is castle where a fearful ogre lives."

"That is the first time the Marquis of Carabas has been called an ogre!" cried the cat.

"What!" exclaimed the King. "Is it not true then, what we have been told about that castle?"

"Sire," returned the cat, "such great wealth and remarkable virtues are bound to arouse envy and malice. If your Majesty will deign to advance, the truth will be made clear!"

"*That's* a good joke," murmured the Marquis of Carabas.

"Better than you know," whispered the cat as he scampered ahead and out of sight.

On the far side of the deep gorge which divided the mountain, Puss met with some workers mowing the flowery grass.

"Harkee, my friends," he said, "the King is coming this way. If he asks you who owns this land, you must answer, 'We and everything else belong to the Marquis of Carabas.' Do this and all will be well. But if you disobey, the ogre will get you."

The mowers promised to remember and obey. Not long afterward, the royal party came cantering by.

"Is this land yours?" asked the King, turning to the miller's son.

"These good folk can inform your Majesty," answered the miller's son.

So the King asked the mowers and they replied all at once, "We and everything else belong to the noble Marquis of Carabas."

"That's a good joke," mumbled the miller's son.

This time the cat was not at hand to make his usual answer. He had run ahead and had already reached the drawbridge of the ogre's great castle.

"Who knocks at my gate?" roared the ogre.

"A traveler, my lord, who has heard of your great gifts and accomplishments," replied the cat.

"Oho," growled the ogre, "in that case, I had better let you in." So the ogre pulled open the gate.

"So you have heard of me?" asked the ogre.

"But I could not believe all that I heard," said the cat. "It is said that your lordship has only to lift up his two thumbs and a banquet spread for three guests will appear."

"That's nothing," cried the ogre, "I need only lift one thumb to do that." So he lifted one thumb and immediately the table appeared.

"Wonderful!" said the cat. "But yet I cannot believe something else that I have heard. I have heard that your lordship can turn himself into any kind of beast."

"That's easy," cried the ogre. "Choose what beast you would like to see."

"An elephant," said the cat. Immediately, the ogre vanished and an elephant stood in his place.

"Most wonderful!" said the cat.

"Would it be too difficult for you to turn into a mouse?" asked the cat. "But perhaps that is something you cannot do?"

"Can't I?" cried the ogre. And in an instant the elephant was gone and a tiny gray mouse ran across the floor. With one blow of his paw, the clever cat killed the mouse and that was the end of Mr. Ogre.

A moment later, there was a knocking at the gate. The royal party had arrived and out ran Puss in Boots to greet them.

"Welcome, O, King! "he cried. "Welcome to the castle of my master, the noble Marquis of Carabas. If your Majesty will deign to follow me," said the cat, "you will find refreshments in the great hall."

"What delightful refreshments," said the King.

"What a beautiful castle," said the Princess.

"Princess," answered the miller's son, "if you wish, the castle and everything in it are yours as much as they are mine."

"That sounds as if you are asking my daughter to marry you," said the King.

"I am," said the miller's son.

"Well, so you shall," declared the King. "If my daughter is willing."

"I am," said the Princess.

So they were married and lived happily in the ogre's castle. And you may be sure that Puss in Boots lived to a happy old age and was given many a saucer of cream by the Marquis and Marquise of Carabas.

The original version of this story was first published in 1697. The illustrations are by an anonymous artist and were first published circa 1890.

Snowdrop

ONCE upon a time, when flakes of snow fell like feathers from the sky, a Queen sat sewing. As she sewed, she thought to herself, "Oh, that I had a child as lovely as these drops of snow." Soon afterwards, she had a little daughter named Snowdrop, but when the child was born, the Queen died.

After a year had gone by, the King took another wife. She was a handsome lady, but she could not stand that anyone should surpass her in beauty. She had a magical mirror, and whenever she walked up to it to look at herself, she said:

"Little glass upon the wall,
Who is fairest of us all?"

And the mirror would reply:

"Lady Queen, so grand and tall,
Thou art fairest of them all."

And the Queen was satisfied, for she knew the mirror never lied. But Snowdrop grew ever fairer, and one day when the Queen asked her mirror, it answered:

"Lady Queen, you are grand and tall,
But Snowdrop is fairest of them all."

Envy grew like weeds in the Queen's heart. So she called a huntsman and said, "Take this child into the forest and kill her."

The huntsman obeyed and led the child away. But when he had drawn his hunting knife, Snowdrop began to weep. The huntsman took pity on her and said, "Run away, then, poor child."

Snowdrop was now all alone in the great, leafy forest. She felt frightened, so she began to run. When evening closed in, she saw a little house and went into it to rest.

Everything in the house was quite small. There stood a little table, on which were seven little plates with seven little places set for dinner. Snowdrop was so very hungry and thirsty that she ate a little of the dinner on each plate and drank a drop from each of the seven little cups.

Along the walls stood seven little beds, and, being very tired, Snowdrop laid herself down upon one of them. The first one was too narrow, and the second one too short. Luckily, the seventh was just right and there Snowdrop fell fast asleep.

Night fell and the seven dwarfs came home. They lit their seven candles, and as soon as they did, they could see that someone had been in the house.

The first said, "Who has been sitting in my chair?"

The second said, "Who has eaten off my plate?"

The third said, "Who has cut with my knife?"

The fourth said, "Who has used my fork?"

The fifth said, "Who has drunk from my cup?"

The sixth said, "Who has been sleeping in my bed?"

But when the seventh dwarf looked in his bed and saw Snowdrop there fast asleep, he cried, "Oh heaven, what a lovely child!"

The seven dwarfs were so pleased that they would not wake her, but let her sleep on. When it was morning, Snowdrop woke up and was frightened to see the seven dwarfs. However, they were very friendly.

"How have you found your way to our house?" they asked.

She told them her sad story, and when she finished, the dwarfs said, "If you will help keep our house, you can stay with us."

So every morning, the dwarfs went to mine the mountain and every evening they came home ready for supper. Since Snowdrop was left alone all day, the good dwarfs warned her, "Your wicked stepmother will soon find out that you are here. Take care that you let no one in."

The Queen, meanwhile, had no doubt that she was the fairest woman in the world. Until one day when she walked up to her mirror and it said:

"Lady Queen, so grand and tall,
Here you are fairest of them all,
But over the hills, with the seven dwarfs old,
Lives Snowdrop, fairer a hundredfold."

Knowing the mirror never told a lie, the Queen pondered how best to kill Snowdrop. Finally, she came up with a plan. She dressed herself like an old peddler and went over the seven hills to where the seven dwarfs dwelt, knocked at the door, and cried, "Good wares, cheap. Very cheap."

Snowdrop looked out the window and called, "Good morning, good woman. What have you to sell?"

"Lovely wares," answered the Queen.

"I may surely let this honest woman in," thought Snowdrop. So she unlocked the door and bought herself a pretty laced bodice.

"Child," said the old woman, "Let me help you." Snowdrop, feared no harm, but the old woman laced so tightly that Snow-drop's breath was stopped, and she fell down as if she were dead.

"Now, I am fairest at last," said the Queen to herself, and she hurried back to the castle.

The seven dwarfs came home soon afterward and they were alarmed to find Snowdrop lifeless on the ground. Seeing that she was laced too tightly, they cut the lace, and Snowdrop slowly returned to life. When the dwarfs heard what had happened, they said, "That old peddler was none other than the wicked Queen. Be careful, Snowdrop, and open the door for no one."

When the cruel Queen reached the castle, she rushed up to her mirror and said:

"Little glass upon the wall,
Who is fairest of us all?"

And the mirror replied:

"Lady Queen, so grand and tall,
Here, you are fairest of them all,
But over the hills, with the seven dwarfs old,
Lives Snowdrop fairer a hundredfold."

This time the Queen made a poisoned comb, changed her clothes, and again she crossed the seven hills. She knocked at the door and cried, "Good wares, very cheap!"

Snowdrop looked out and said, "Go away, I dare let no one in."

"You may surely be allowed to look," answered the old woman as she drew out the poisoned comb. Snowdrop thought the comb was so beautiful that she opened the door.

The old woman said, "Let me fix your hair properly." The comb scarcely touched Snowdrop's hair before the poison worked and Snowdrop fell down senseless.

Snowdrop

Luckily, it was near evening and the seven dwarfs soon came home. When they found Snowdrop, they searched her until they found the poisoned comb. As soon as they had drawn it out of her hair, Snowdrop came to and told them what had happened. Again, they warned her to be careful.

Once more, the Queen rushed to her mirror and said:
> "Little glass upon the wall,
> Who is fairest of us all?"

And, once more, the mirror answered:
> "Lady Queen, so grand and tall,
> Here you are fairest of them all,
> But over the hills, with seven dwarfs old,
> Lives Snowdrop fairer a thousandfold."

When the Queen heard the mirror speak, she quivered with rage. "Snowdrop shall die," she cried, " even if it costs me my own life!" Then she went to a secret chamber and made an apple of deadly poison. When the apple was ready, the Queen again disguised herself and journeyed to where the dwarfs lived.

At the sound of the knock, Snowdrop said, "I cannot open the door."

"I only want to be rid of my apples," replied the peddlar woman. "Here, I will give you one."

"No!" said Snowdrop. "I cannot take it."

"Look here," said the old woman, "there's nothing wrong with this apple. I will cut it in two, and you can have the rosy side."

Now the apple was so cleverly made that only the rosy side was poisoned. Snowdrop longed for the apple and when she saw the old woman eating one half, she could resist no longer. Scarcely had Snowdrop tasted it, than she fell lifeless to the ground.

When the Queen got home, she asked the mirror who was the fairest in the land, and the mirror answered:
> "Lady Queen, so grand and tall,
> You are the fairest of them all."

And so the Queen's jealous heart was as much at rest as a jealous heart can be.

When the dwarfs came home, they again found Snowdrop on the ground. They lifted her up, searched her, unlaced her, combed her hair, but all was useless. Finally, they laid her on a bier and mourned her for three long days. They would have buried her, but she looked so much like she was sleeping that they couldn't bring themselves to do it. Instead, they made a coffin of glass and laid her in it. Then they placed the coffin on the mountain above and one of the dwarfs stood by it day and night. But there was little need to guard it, for even the wild animals came to mourn for Snowdrop.

Many, many long years did Snowdrop lie unchanged. At last, a prince wandered into the forest. He saw the coffin on the mountain and said to the dwarfs, "If you will let me have the coffin, I will give you whatever you wish."

But the dwarfs answered, "We would not part with it for all the gold in the world."

So the prince begged them again, "Please let me take her home with me, for I cannot live without seeing Snowdrop every day."

The prince spoke with such sincerity that the good dwarfs took pity on him and gave him the coffin. He had it carried away by his servants, who happened to stumble along the way. The bump forced the poisoned apple out of Snowdrop's throat. Immediately, she opened her eyes and sat up.

"Where am I?" she asked.

The Prince answered joyfully, saying "From the moment I saw you, I have loved you. Will you come with me to my father's castle and be my wife?"

Snowdrop was well pleased with this invitation and went with him gladly.

The day of the wedding feast, the wicked Queen stood before her mirror once more and asked:

> "Little glass upon the wall,
> Who is fairest of them all?"

The mirror answered:

> "Lady Queen, so grand and tall,
> Here you are fairest of them all,
> But the young Queen over the mountain old,
> Is fairer than you a thousandfold."

The Queen uttered an evil curse, but curiosity would not allow her to rest. She determined to travel and see who this young queen could be. When she arrived at the castle and found that it was Snowdrop, she stood petrified with terror. Then two iron shoes were laid before her, and she was forced to put them on and to dance at Snowdrop's wedding—dancing and dancing in those heavy shoes until she fell down dead. And that was the end of her.

The original version of this story was first published in 1812. The illustrations are by W. C. Drupsteen and were first published circa 1885.

The Frog Prince

ONE fine evening, a young princess sat by the side of a cool spring of water. She had a golden ball in her hand and she amused herself by tossing it into the air and catching it as it fell. After a time she threw it up so high that when she stretched out her hand to catch it, the ball bounded away and rolled along, till at last it fell into the spring.

The Princess looked into the spring, but it was very deep, so deep that she could not see the bottom of it. Then she began to cry and said, "Alas! If I could only get my ball again, I would give all my fine clothes and jewels and everything that I have in the world."

While she was crying, a frog poked its head out of the water and said "Princess, why do you weep so bitterly?"

"Alas!" said she. "What can you do for me, you ugly frog? My golden ball has fallen into the spring."

The frog said, "I want not your pearls and jewels and fine clothes, but if you will love me and let me live with you and eat from your little golden plate and sleep upon your little bed, I will bring you your ball."

"What nonsense!" thought the Princess. "He can never get out of the spring. However, he may be able to get my ball for me, and therefore I will promise him what he asks." So she said to the frog, "If you will bring me my ball, I promise to do all you ask." Then the frog dove deep under the water.

After a little while, he came up again with the ball in his

mouth. As soon as the young Princess saw her ball, she ran to pick it up, and was so overjoyed to have it in her hand again that she never even thought of the frog, but ran home with the ball as fast as she could. The frog called after her, "Stay, Princess, and take me with you as you promised." But the Princess did not stop to hear a word.

The next day, just as the Princess had sat down to dinner, she heard a strange noise, tap-tap-tap, as if somebody was coming up the marble staircase. Then, something knocked gently at the door.

The Princess ran to the door and opened it, and there she saw

the frog. She was terribly frightened, and, shutting the door as fast as she could, she returned to her seat. The King, her father, asked her what had frightened her. "There is a nasty frog," she said, "at

the door, who lifted my ball out of the spring yesterday. I promised him that he should live with me here, thinking that he could never get out of the spring, but there he is at the door and wants to come in!" While she was speaking the frog knocked again at the door.

The King said to the young Princess, "As you have made a promise, you must keep it. Go and let him in." She did so, and the frog hopped into the room, and came up close to the table.

"Pray lift me upon a chair," said he to the Princess, "and let me sit next to you." As soon as she had done this, the frog said "Put your plate closer to me that I may eat out of it." This she did, and when he had eaten as much as he could, he said, "Now I am tired. Carry me upstairs and put me into your little bed." And the Prin-

cess took him up in her hand and put him upon the pillow of her own little bed, where he slept all night long.

As soon as it was light he jumped up, hopped downstairs, and went out of the house. "Now," thought the Princess, "he is gone, and I shall be troubled with him no more."

But she was mistaken, for when night came again, she heard the same tapping at the door. When she opened it, the frog came in and slept upon her pillow as before until morning. The third night he did the same, but when the Princess awoke the following morning, she was astonished to see, instead of the frog, a handsome prince standing at the head of her bed.

He told her that he had been enchanted by an evil fairy, who had changed him into a frog, and so he would have had to remain unless a princess should take him out of the spring and let him sleep upon her bed for three nights. "You," said the Prince, "have broken this cruel charm, and now I have nothing to wish for but that you should go with me into my father's kingdom, where I will marry you and love you as long as I live."

The young Princess, you may be sure, was not long in giving her consent, and as they spoke a splendid carriage drove up. It was driven by eight beautiful horses decked with plumes of feathers and a golden harness, and behind rode the Prince's servant, the faithful Henry, who had bewailed the misfortune of his dear master so long and bitterly that his heart had well-nigh burst. Then all set out full of joy for the Prince's kingdom, where they arrived safely and lived happily a great many years.

The original version of this story was first published in 1812. The illustrations are by Walter Crane and were first published in 1874.

Beauty
and
the Beast

THERE once lived a merchant who owned a great fleet of ships. He was proud of these ships, but prouder yet of his daughters. The eldest was fair, the second even more so, but the youngest was so lovely that people called her "Beauty."

One year, great tempests scattered the merchant's ships. Thus, the merchant went from being very rich to being very poor. He sold his mansion and went to live in a tiny cottage.

The two elder sisters did not meet with this sudden change of fortune bravely, but Beauty ignored her own troubles and set out to help her father. She did all the work of the cottage and was always merry. It seemed that her name suited her better every day.

At last, news came that one of the ships had cast anchor in a distant seaport and the merchant was summoned to claim it. He called his daughters to him and said, "Dear children, we shall never be rich again, but perhaps we may be a bit less poor. I do not want to return to you empty-handed, so choose what you would like me to bring you." The eldest asked for a string of pearls; the second for a pair of ruby earrings.

"And I," said Beauty, "would like a rose plant for my garden."

When he reached the seaport, the merchant learned that the ship had been almost completely ruined and he could only afford to buy wooden beads and glass earrings for his daughters.

"Luckily," he said to himself, "I shall not have to disappoint Beauty. It should be no hard matter to find a rose bush." But he

soon found that it was a very hard matter indeed. He could have tulips and lilies by the dozen, but not a rose could be found.

"Alas," said the merchant, "I shall have to disappoint my Beauty after all."

The road home wound through a dark forest. Toward nightfall, the merchant began to realize that he had lost his way. Where he had expected to find an inn, he found only tangled trees. Still, he pushed ahead and soon he saw a twinkling of light.

It was not long before he reached the gates of a house. The gates were ajar, so he led his horse up the drive. Though he shouted at the top of his voice, no one answered. The door was open and the merchant could see that lamps were lit and a bright fire burned in the hearth. The merchant hesitated, but it was growing late, so he decided to tether his horse and sit by the fire until someone should appear.

When he returned from the stable, he was amazed to see that a tempting supper had been set forth. Again he hesitated, but he was very hungry and the supper smelled very good, so he sat down

and enjoyed the meal. After supper, the merchant began to feel
sleepy. Through a half-open door he could see a bed. He lay down
and by the time he woke up, the sun was shining and breakfast had
been laid in the hall. Full of astonishment, the merchant ate. Then
he went to fetch his horse, which he found groomed and saddled.
He led his horse down the drive, calling out thanks for all the
kindness he had received. Just as he was about to ride away, he
caught sight of a magnificent rose bush. Remembering his promise
to Beauty, he decided to cut just one flower. But no sooner had his
knife touched the rose than he heard a terrible roar and a most
fearsome-looking creature appeared.

Beauty and the Beast

"Is this your gratitude?" asked the Beast. "I treated you as an honored guest, and you repay me by stealing that which I love more than anything else."

"Sir," said the poor merchant, trembling, "If I had known, I would not have laid a finger on the rose. But I promised my daughter a rose and I did not want to disappoint her."

"You love your daughter very much then?" asked the Beast.

"Truly, Sir, I do," answered the merchant. "She is not only beautiful, but she has the kindest heart in the world."

"*Hum*," growled the Beast, "I will let you go, provided that you promise me that within seven days you will either return or send this daughter of yours in your stead."

The poor merchant sorrowfully gave his word.

"Take the rose," said the Beast, "and this bag of gold. In seven days I shall be standing here. Woe to you and yours, if neither you nor your daughter should come by that day."

When the merchant reached home, his daughters ran out to meet him. The two elder ones jumped for joy when they saw the bag of gold dangling from the saddle, but their joy turned to sadness when they heard of his strange adventure.

"Do not weep, my children," said the merchant, "I ought not to have touched those roses."

"Dearest father," whispered Beauty, "it was my fault. I will go in your place."

"Never!" cried her father.

"I will go," repeated Beauty. "Perhaps the Beast will not kill *me*. Poor Beast. He must be very sad."

Nothing that her father or her sisters could say would change Beauty's mind. When the seventh day came, she kissed them all farewell and set off on her journey.

Though the Beast had said that he would be waiting at the gate, Beauty saw nobody when she arrived. She led her horse into the stable and then tiptoed into the house, dreading at every moment to see the fearsome face of the Beast.

She was surprised to find a door marked "Beauty's Room." When she opened it she found herself in a lovely room filled with tapestries. There was a silver cage full of bullfinches and canaries in one corner and a golden harp in another and in the center stood a rose bush in a great bronze pot.

"It seems," thought Beauty, "that I am not to be gobbled up after all!"

In one of the outer rooms she found a dainty supper laid for one. "I suppose," she thought, "the poor Beast always has to eat alone."

Beauty and the Beast

Hardly had she finished her supper, when the door opened and the Beast came slowly into the room. Beauty uttered a cry, for he really was a fearsome Beast. But she soon saw that she had no reason to fear, for the expression on his shaggy face was sad rather than fierce.

"You are afraid of me," said the Beast, in a gruff voice.

"Not now," returned Beauty, gently.

"Are you willing," asked the Beast, "to spend a year in this house, to save your father? If the sight of me is terrible to you, I can look at you from a distance. That will be enough for me."

The next day when Beauty was in the garden, she caught sight of the Beast hidden among the trees. He looked so sad that she called out, "Sir Beast, I have something I wish to say to you!"

The Beast came eagerly forward. "I am afraid I must have hurt you last night," said Beauty, "when I agreed to stay here only if you kept out of my sight. Perhaps you would like to come and talk to me sometimes when I walk in the garden."

"I should like it very much," returned the Beast. "I never have anybody to talk to."

A week passed and every morning Beauty and the Beast strolled about the garden. Beauty was surprised to find that her host could be a most interesting companion.

"Were you playing the harp last night, Beauty?" the Beast asked one morning.

"Yes," said Beauty, "but I soon got tired of playing as there was no one to listen."

"May I listen outside the door?" asked the Beast.

"Of course you may," said Beauty.

The next day, when she began to play she heard footsteps outside the door and called out, "You could hear better if you came in, Sir Beast!"

So the Beast came in, looking so delighted that for the moment she almost forgot that he was a Beast at all.

After a little while, Beauty began to wonder how her father

and sisters were. The Beast soon saw that she was fretting. When she told him why, he brought her a round bronze mirror.

"This mirror," he said, "will tell you what you want to know."

Beauty gazed into the mirror, and there she saw her father weeping. As the days passed, Beauty became more and more anxious about her father. At last the Beast said to her, "Dear Beauty, I will not keep you here when your heart is elsewhere. You can go whenever you wish."

"Can I go tomorrow?" asked Beauty.

"Today, if you wish," returned the Beast.

But he spoke so sadly that she said, "Tomorrow will be soon enough."

When she said these words two tears gathered in the Beast's eyes and rolled down his shaggy cheeks.

"I love you so, dear Beauty," said the Beast, "that when you leave my heart will break. But I love you too much to keep you here, where you must be very unhappy."

"Not so," answered Beauty, gently. "I have spent many happy hours here with you, Sir Beast, and I shall often remember them. But my father is so sad without me, that I must go to him."

"That is very natural," sighed the Beast.

The next morning when Beauty set off for home, she was surprised that the Beast did not come out to bid her good-bye. The poor Beast was, in truth, too heartbroken. But he watched her from a distance and saw her wave farewell to the garden before she passed through the iron gates and disappeared from sight.

The merchant and his two elder daughters were greatly astonished when Beauty returned. Hardly had she begun to tell her story, when four men arrived with a huge leather trunk. On the lid was a label: *To Beauty, from the Beast.* The sisters uttered loud cries of delight when they saw what treasures were within. At the very bottom of the heap lay the bronze mirror.

"I will hang that on the wall of my room," said Beauty.

For a few days Beauty was so glad to be at home again that she almost forgot about the Beast. But soon she began to think

about him. Tunes that she used to play to him on the harp would come suddenly into her mind, or when she began to read a book she would remember that the Beast had read it and had told her about it. Then one day she suddenly remembered the mirror. She ran upstairs and took it down from the wall. In it she saw a corner of the Beast's garden. The Beast was lying on the grass weeping.

"My *poor* Beast!" cried Beauty.

She slipped away, saddled her horse, and galloped until she reached the Beast's house. Then she ran from room to room, calling him, but all was silent. So Beauty ran to the garden. There she found the poor Beast lying, almost lifeless.

At the sound of Beauty's voice, the Beast tried to rise, but he was too weak. So she knelt beside him and lifted his shaggy head on her arm. Then he opened his eyes and said faintly, "Beauty, why have you come back to me?"

"Because I love you," said Beauty.

She bent to kiss him. But even though she loved him, she had to shut her eyes, because he was so fearful to behold.

"Look at me, dear Beauty," said the Beast.

Beauty opened her eyes and saw that he was a Beast no longer.

"Dear Beauty," he said, "I was doomed by a wicked fairy to wear the mask of a monster and to live a life of sorrow and loneliness until someone should love me despite my terrible looks. Only by a kiss could I be freed. Your compassion has broken the spell."

When the merchant received a letter from Beauty bidding him to receive her and her husband, he was much astonished and not a little alarmed. His elder daughters screamed at the very idea of receiving a Beast as a brother-in-law.

You can just imagine their surprise and delight when they found that he was not such a beast after all!

The original version of this story was first published in 1756. The illustrations are by M. Bowley and were first published circa 1920.

The Princess
and
the Pea

ONCE upon a time, there was a prince who wanted to marry a princess, but only a *real* princess would do. So he set off around the world to find one. There were plenty of princesses, but he could never be certain that they were really, truly princesses. There was always something that did not seem quite right: this one was too tall; that one too short; this one too stupid; that one too vain. And so he returned home, very sad indeed, for he wanted more than anything to find a real princess who could rule his kingdom with him.

One evening there was a terrible storm. There was roaring thunder and flashing lightning. The rain poured in torrents. It was a frightening storm, and in the middle of it, there was a knock at the door. The King himself went to open it and when he did, he found a princess. Or at least she said she was a princess. Her hair and clothes were soaking wet and she was nearly blue from the cold. But, nonetheless, she insisted she was a *real* princess and so the King let her in.

The Queen, however, wasn't so sure she was a real princess, so she ordered that a bed be prepared for the unknown guest. The servants piled twenty mattresses, one on top of the other, and then they added twenty blankets. At the very bottom of all this, the Queen secretly placed a solitary pea. Then she wished the princess a good night's rest and everyone set off to sleep.

The next morning, the Queen asked the Princess how she slept.

The Princess and the Pea

"Quite dreadfully," replied the Princess. "I hardly slept a wink all night, for there was a terrible lump in my mattress. I'm black and blue all over. I don't know what it could have been."

Now the Queen knew that indeed this princess was a true princess, because only a true princess could feel a pea through twenty mattresses. So the Prince married the Princess and ordered that the pea be placed in a royal museum. And, as far as anyone knows, it's still there today.

The original version of this story was first published in 1836. The illustrations are by Kay Nielsen and were first published in 1924.

Jack and the Beanstalk

THERE once lived a poor widow who had a son called Jack. He was not a bad boy, but he thought that it was far better fun to fish or to go hunting for blackberries than to chop wood or weed the garden.

One day, Jack's mother looked so sad that he asked her what was the matter.

"Alas," said the poor woman, "I have no more money. I shall have to sell our cow."

Jack was sorry to hear that the cow must be sold, but he was very anxious to be allowed to sell her himself.

"Please, Mother," he urged, "let *me* sell her."

Reluctantly, the widow agreed, and away went Jack with the cow.

Jack had not gone very far before he met a peddler who was carefully carrying his hat.

"The sun is hot," said Jack. "Why don't you wear your hat upon your head?"

"Because," replied the peddler, "I have something in my hat that I prize far more than my head."

Jack peeped into the hat, but all he could see was a heap of beans.

"Did you ever see beans such as these?" asked the peddler.

"No," returned Jack. "What are you going to do with them? Are you going to boil them? Or are you going to plant them in the ground?"

"Neither. I am going to sell them for some gold."

Jack began to think that there must be something very unusual about these beans.

"Harkee," said Jack, "I have no money, but I am on my way to sell this beautiful cow. When I have sold her, I should like to buy those beans of yours."

"Why wait till then?" replied the peddler. "I will take the cow in exchange."

Jack agreed and away went the peddler with the cow and away ran Jack, eager to tell his mother how clever he had been. But when he spread the beans out on the table and told her what he had done, she burst into tears.

"I am ruined," she sobbed.

"Wait a minute, mother," he said, "these are not ordinary beans. Look!"

"I *won't* look!" cried Jack's mother. Then she jumped up and threw the beans out the window.

The next morning the sun seemed very late in rising. Jack opened his eyes three times and three times he shut them again, because his little room was still dark. The *fourth* time, he sat up in surprise for he saw that the darkness was not black or gray, but *green*. He ran to the window and found that it was completely blocked by a gigantic beanstalk dangling with huge green leaves. Evidently they were *not* ordinary beans after all!

A moment later, Jack was out in the garden and gazing up at the marvelous plant.

"I'm going up!" said Jack to himself.

Jack was a skillful climber, but by the time he reached the top, he was out of breath.

As far as the eye could see, stretched a vast plain of silvery-white sand. The boy's first impulse was to clamber back *down* the beanstalk as fast as he had clambered *up* it. Then, curiosity caused him to change his mind.

So he rose from his perch on the cloud and began to walk across the white sand. He went *on* and *on* and *on*, but never a

cottage nor a tree nor a hedge did he see. Just when he was beginning to lose heart, he saw the towers of a great castle in the distance.

Jack had never seen a castle before, but he thought that it looked like the sort of place where there would be plenty to eat and drink, so he quickened his footsteps. Soon he reached the iron-barred door, at which he knocked.

After a few moments, the door swung back and a large face peered out. It was a giantess.

"Who's there?" asked the giantess.

"Please, your Ladyship," Jack said politely, "I am only a poor boy. Will you not give me something to eat?"

The giantess liked being called "your Ladyship." So she beckoned to Jack.

"Come in," she said, "but if my husband comes home, you must hide yourself at once. There is nothing he likes better than roasted boy."

This sounded alarming, but Jack followed the giantess into the castle. Just as he finished eating, the floor began to quake and the cups and saucers began to rattle. The giantess cried out, "Oh, here comes my husband! Creep into the closet, boy, and when he falls asleep you can slip away."

Jack crept hastily into the closet. A moment later the giant came striding into the kitchen, roaring:

"Fee, fi, fo, fum—
I smell the blood of an Englishman!"

"Nothing of the sort," returned the giantess. "What you smell is a roast pig."

Jack remained very quiet in the closet till the giant had finished his supper. But then, he could not resist the temptation to open the door and peep through the crack.

"Wife," said the giant, "bring me my hen."

The giantess disappeared and soon returned, carrying a hen with golden feathers. This hen she placed on the table before her husband, who roared the one word, "Lay!"

And the hen promptly laid an egg. But it was not an ordinary egg. Jack could see that it was made of solid gold.

After the hen had laid six or seven eggs, the giant and the giantess became drowsy and before long they were both snoring like the very deepest thunder. Then Jack crept out of the oven, tucked the pretty little golden hen under his arm, and ran for his life. Across the white sand he ran until he came to the place where the green leaves of the beanstalk pushed up through the clouds. Then down he clambered, as fast as he could, keeping the hen tucked under his arm all the time.

You may imagine how glad the poor widow was to see her boy again.

"Look, mother," said Jack, "I have brought you a hen to make up for the loss of our good old cow!"

"It is a pretty hen," returned Jack's mother, "but I will wait and see whether it is a good layer before I stop grieving for my cow."

Jack set the hen upon the table. "Lay!" said he.

And at once the hen laid a golden egg.

For a time, Jack and his mother lived very contentedly upon the money which they made by selling the eggs of the giant's pretty little hen. Then Jack was seized with a great desire to pay another visit to the castle in the clouds.

So Jack clambered up the beanstalk again and soon found his way to the giant's castle, where he knocked boldly at the door.

"Who's there?" asked the giantess, peering out. "If it's the same rascal of a human boy that came before, you had better be off!"

"Your Highness," said Jack, "if *I* had annoyed you in any way, do you think I should dare to come back again?"

The giantess liked being called "your Highness." She remarked. "At first, I thought you *were* the boy who stole my husband's pretty little hen. But as you are *not* he, you may come in."

Jack followed her into the kitchen, where she gave him a piece of gingerbread nearly as big as a haystack. When he had nibbled off one corner, the floor began to quake and the cups began to rattle and the giant's voice was heard roaring:

"*Fee, fi, fo, fum* —
I smell the blood of an Englishman!"
Jack hurriedly crept into a big chest. The giantess assured her husband that what he smelled was a roast goose.

When the giant had devoured the goose he said, "Wife, bring me my moneybags!"

The giantess then brought him two large sacks full of golden coins. While she had a nap by the fire, he amused himself by letting the money run through his huge fingers. Then the giant became sleepy, tied up the two bags, and began to snore. As soon as he heard the giant's thundering snore, Jack softly raised the lid of the chest and got out. Seizing a bag of coins under each arm, he ran for his life. When he reached the top of the beanstalk he realized that he could not possibly climb down with such a heavy load. So he opened the sacks and poured the coins down through the clouds.

The widow was amazed to see money showering down from the sky. The moment Jack reached the ground, she swore that he must *never* climb the beanstalk again. But Jack only laughed, for in his own mind he had resolved to visit the giant's castle just *once* more.

A few days later, when his mother had gone into the town to do some shopping, Jack swung himself up the beanstalk. He knocked at the giant's door for the third time.

Jack and the Beanstalk

"Go away," the giantess roared through the keyhole. "No boys must come here, unless they wish to be eaten!"

"Your Grace," returned Jack, "I am not a boy. I am an old man!"

And indeed the mischievous fellow had tied a huge beard of white wool to his chin.

The giantess, who liked being called "your Grace," slowly opened the door.

Jack entered the kitchen and listened politely while she told him about the two wicked boys who had stolen the giant's treasures.

"All boys are rogues and rascals!" declared Jack, solemnly wagging his beard.

Then the ground began to quake and the cups began to rattle.

"Oh!" cried the giantess, "Here comes my husband! Hide, old man, hide in the clock!"

Jack squeezed himself into the tall clock and a moment later the giant himself came stomping in, growling:

"Fee, fi, fo, fum—
I smell the blood of an Englishman!"

"No, you don't," said the giantess. "What you smell is a joint of beef, which is cooking for your supper."

It did not take the giant long to devour the beef. When he had finished, he said, "Alas, my pretty hen is gone and my bags of money are gone, but I have one treasure left. Wife, bring me my harp!"

The giantess brought forth a beautiful golden harp that began to play the most lovely music. Very soon both she and the giant were lulled to sleep. Then Jack leapt out of the clock, snatched the harp from the table, and ran for his life. But at the touch of Jack's hand the harp began to cry, "Master, master!"

Up jumped the giant, rubbing his eyes, and away dashed Jack as fast as he could go.

Jack and the Beanstalk

"Rogue, rascal, thief!" roared the giant. "Wait till I catch you!"

As swiftly as a deer, Jack sped over the white sand to the place where the green leaves of the beanstalk pushed up through the clouds. The harp continued to make music and the giant continued to roar after Jack.

"Mother, mother," called Jack, "bring me a hatchet, quick!"

Out ran Jack's mother with a big hatchet in her hand.

As soon as he reached the ground, her son began to chop the beanstalk. Just as the giant reached the top, Jack's hatchet sliced right through the stalk. When he saw that he could not possibly climb down the broken beanstalk, the giant uttered a furious roar and went back to his castle, howling all the way.

The roots of the beanstalk withered away, and, as Jack had not kept any seeds, it could not be planted again. But the pretty little hen continued to lay golden eggs for them, and the fairy harp made music for them whenever they told it to play, and so Jack and his mother lived happily ever after.

The original version of this story was first published in 1734. The illustrations are by John Hassall and were first published in 1904.

Snow White and Rose Red

A poor widow lived in a cottage, in front of which stood two little rose trees: one with red roses, the other with white. The widow had two children, who resembled these rose trees: one was called Snow White, the other Rose Red. They were so gentle that even the creatures of the wood were not afraid of them. The little hare ate cabbage leaves out of their hands, the doe grazed at their sides, the stag sprang merrily past them, and when they were near, the birds never ceased their songs.

Every summer morning, Rose Red gathered a nosegay for her mother in which was a rose from each tree. In winter, Snow White lit the fire and in the evening they would sit by the hearth. The mother would take out her spectacles, and she would read from a book as the two girls listened. Near them lay a lamb on the floor and perched behind them was a little white dove with its head tucked under its wing.

One evening as they were reading, someone knocked at the door. Rose Red went and pushed the bolt back. At first she thought it was a poor man, seeking shelter, but it turned out to be a bear. Rose Red screamed, the little lamb bleated, the dove fluttered about, and Snow White hid herself behind her mother's bed. But the bear began to speak.

"Do not be frightened. I will do you no harm," he said. "I am half frozen and only want to warm myself."

"You poor bear," said the mother. "Lay yourself down before the fire." Then she called out, "Snow White, Rose Red, come out. The bear means you no harm."

Slowly the two girls came out of their hiding places. The bear said, "Children, knock the snow out of my fur. I am freezing." So they fetched a broom, and they swept the bear's fur clean. Then he stretched himself before the fire and growled softly, like a bear that was quite happy.

In a short time, they all became friends. The children enjoyed playing with their guest. They rubbed their feet on his back and scratched his ears with a hazel rod. The bear was very pleased with all this play, but now and then when the children became too mischievous, he would say, "Lovely Snow White; lovely Rose Red, you will strike your beloved dead."

When bedtime came, the children went to sleep and the mother said to the bear, "You can lie on the hearth so you will be sheltered from the cold."

Henceforward, the bear came every evening at the same hour and laid himself on the hearth. The children became so used to him that the door was never bolted until their companion arrived.

When spring came, the bear said to Snow White, "Now I must go away and may not come again the whole summer."

"Where are you going, dear Bear?" asked Snow White.

"I must go far into the woods and guard my treasures from the gnomes. In winter when the ground is frozen hard, they must stay underneath. But now that the sun has thawed the earth, they break through and come up and steal. What is once in their hands does not come so easily into daylight again."

Snow White was quite sorrowful at the parting, but she went to open the door for him. As she unbolted the door and the bear ran out, the hook of the door caught a piece of his skin and tore it off. It seemed to Snow White that she had seen gold shining through, but the bear ran quickly away and soon disappeared behind the trees.

After some time, the mother sent the children into the woods to collect kindling. They found a large tree which had been cut down. Something was jumping up and down by the trunk, but they could not tell what it was. As they came nearer, they saw it was a gnome with a long beard. The end of it was stuck in the tree and the little fellow was jumping about trying to get the beard free. He stared at the girls with his fiery red eyes and screamed, "Why are you just standing there? Do something!"

The children tried and tried, but they could not pull the beard out. "I will run and fetch somebody," said Rose Red.

"You foolish ninny," snarled the gnome. "You are already two too many for me. Can't you think of anything better?"

"Don't be so impatient," said Snow White. "I have an idea." Then she took a little pair of scissors from her pocket and cut the end of his beard off.

As soon as the gnome was free, he seized a sack filled with gold that was sticking between the roots of the tree. Pulling it out, he growled, "You rude people cut off a piece of my beautiful beard! May evil reward you." Then he threw the sack over his shoulders and walked way without once looking back.

Some time later, Snow White and Rose Red went to catch some fish for dinner. As they neared the stream, they saw something jumping on the bank. When they got closer, they recognized the gnome. The little fellow had been fishing and the line had gotten tangled in his beard. A great fish bit at his hook, and the gnome was in imminent danger of being drowned.

The girls had arrived just in time. They held him tight and tried to untangle the line, but his beard and line were tangled fast together. There was nothing to do but pull out the scissors again. When the gnome saw this, he cried out, "Is that manners, you goose? Is it not enough that you have already ruined my beard, now you have cut off the best part as well?" Then, he fetched a sack of pearls that lay among the rushes, and without saying a word, he dragged it away and disappeared behind a stone.

Soon after, the mother sent the girls to town. The road led them by a heath, where they saw an eagle hovering in the air. It circled round and round and at last settled by a rock. Instantly, they heard a wailing cry. They ran up and saw that the eagle had seized the gnome. The children quickly grabbed hold of the little man and tugged and tugged. They struggled so long that the eagle finally let go.

When the gnome had recovered from his fright, he called out in a shrill voice, "Couldn't you have been more gentle? You awkward, clumsy creatures have torn my coat into tatters." Then he took a sack of gems and slipped behind a rock into his den. The girls were used to his ingratitude by now, and they continued on their way to town.

As they were coming home, they came upon the gnome again. He had emptied his sacks on the ground, not thinking that anyone would come by there so late. The evening sun shone on the glittering treasure, and it looked so beautiful that the children could not help but stare.

"Why do you stand there gaping?" cried the gnome, his face turning red with anger. Suddenly, they heard a loud roar, and a bear trotted out of the woods. The gnome sprang up terrified, but the bear was already close upon him.

Snow White and Rose Red

The gnome called out, "Dear Mr. Bear, spare me and you shall have all my treasures. Look at the beautiful stones that lie there. Give me my life! What do you want with a poor thin fellow like me? You would scarcely feel me between your teeth. Rather seize those two wicked girls. They will be tender morsels, for they are as fat as young quails."

The bear didn't answer, but instead gave the malicious creature a single stroke with his paw, and the little gnome did not move again. The girls had run away, but the bear called after them, "Snow White! Rose Red! Wait, I will go with you."

Recognizing the voice of their old friend, the girls stopped. When the bear caught up with them, his fur suddenly fell off. Behold, he was not a bear, but a handsome young man dressed all in gold.

"I am a king's son," he said. "That wicked gnome stole all my treasure and changed me into a wild bear. I have been obliged to run about in the woods until I should be freed by his death. Now, he has received his well-deserved punishment."

So they all went home to the widow's cottage. Snow White was married to the prince and Rose Red to his brother. They divided between them the great treasure which the gnome had amassed. The old mother left the cottage to live with her children in the palace, but she took the two rose trees with her and every year they bore the most beautiful roses: one white, the other red.

The original version of this story was first published in 1812. The illustrations are by Hermann Vogel-Planen, and were first published in 1894.

Tom Thumb

LONG ago, there lived a ploughman and his wife. They were very poor, but they longed for nothing more than a child of their very own.

"How happy I should be if I had but one child," said the wife. "Even if it were only as big as my thumb, I would love it dearly."

Now it came to pass, that this good woman's wish was fulfilled. Some time afterward, she had a little boy who was quite healthy and strong, but not much bigger than a thumb. So they said, "Well, we cannot say we have not gotten what we wished for, and little as he is, we will love him dearly." They named him Tom Thumb.

Now Tom lived happily with his parents until one day, when he was sitting with his mother in the kitchen. His mother was mixing a delicious pudding and when her back was turned, Tom fell into the bowl. His mother was so busy, that she didn't notice. She stirred Tom right into the pudding and then poured it into a pot. No sooner did this happen than Tom started to kick and yell and jump. He made such a commotion that his mother, thinking that the pudding was bewitched, was nearly frightened out of her wits. She grabbed the pudding pot, ran with it to the door, and gave it to a tinker who was passing by.

The tinker was grateful to have the pudding and was looking forward to a finer treat than he had had in many a long day, when he sneezed very hard. Tom called out, "Bless you!" as loud as he could. This so terrified the tinker that he flung the pudding into some bushes and ran away as fast as he could.

Tom crept out of the bushes covered with batter and ran home to his mother, who had been looking everywhere for him. She was delighted to see him and gave him a bath in a cup, and Tom was none the worse for his adventure.

A few days after this, Tom went with his mother into the fields to milk the cows. Fearing that the wind might blow the little boy away, she tied him to a sturdy flower with a piece of silken thread. While Tom's mother was off a cow came by, bit off the flower, and swallowed up poor Tom.

Tom Thumb

Tom called out loudly, "Mother! Mother!" His mother looked everywhere, but she could not find him. Finally, Tom began to kick and scratch until the cow spit him out of her mouth. On seeing this, his mother rushed to him, took him up in her arms, and carried him safely home.

Some days after this, Tom's father took him out to the fields to do some ploughing. He gave Tom a whip made of barley straw and Tom set to work. But the field was big and Tom was soon lost in a furrow. An eagle saw him walking about on the ground and snatched him up. He flew away with poor Tom, across the fields, over the hills, to the edge of the sea. All the while, Tom was kicking and yelling, and this so tired the eagle that it finally gave up its struggle to hold onto its prey and dropped Tom into the sea.

Scarcely had Tom touched the water before he was swallowed by a large fish, which was caught shortly afterwards and offered to the King. When the fish was opened, everyone was astonished to find little Tom inside. The King was especially astonished and he immediately made Tom the Court's official Little Knight.

Tom Thumb

Tom quickly grew to enjoy life at the Court, but he always missed his parents and so one day, he begged the King's permission to go home for a visit. The King quickly agreed and gave Tom a small purse of golden coins to take with him.

Tom had to rest more than a thousand times along the way, but he finally reached home. His mother and father ran out to meet him and there was great rejoicing at his arrival. After a lengthy visit, Tom decided to return to Court once more. He gave his mother and father the purse filled with gold, promised them he'd visit again soon, and then set off on his long journey.

He had almost reached the Court, when he became so tired that he couldn't take another step, so he crawled into an empty flower pot for a nap. When he awoke, he peeped out. Seeing a butterfly on the ground nearby, he stole out of his hiding place, jumped on the butterfly's back, and took off into the air.

When he arrived at the Court, he called out to everyone that he had returned. The King and all the nobles all ran about trying to catch the butterfly, so that Tom could join them once more, but none succeeded. Finally, Tom fell from the butterfly into a watering can, where he would have drowned had not the royal Princess pulled him out. The King was so pleased to have his little friend back, that he declared a week of feasting.

Tom lived for many years at the King's Court and became known far and wide as one of the most beloved of all the King's knights.

The original version of this story was first published in 1621. The illustrations are by L. Leslie Brooke and were first published in 1904.

Cinderella

LONG ago there lived a widower who had one daughter. For his second wife, he chose a widow who had two daughters. All three had very jealous natures, which was unfortunate for the gentleman's daughter, because they made her stay at home and do all the hard work while they put on their finest dresses and went to garden parties. Her only refuge when all the work was done was the kitchen hearth and so her stepsisters nicknamed her "Cinderella." But with her faded cotton dress and ribbonless hair, Cinderella looked a thousand times more lovely than her two wicked stepsisters did when they wore their brightest silks and a whole rainbow of ribbons in their hair.

When they heard that the King's only son was going to give two magnificent balls, the stepsisters quickly put poor Cinderella to work. For weeks she slaved, starching and ironing, embroidering and sewing. At last, the evening arrived and after the stepsisters drove away, Cinderella sat down beside the hearth and burst into tears.

Suddenly, she heard a voice say, "What is the matter, my poor child?" And to her astonishment, Cinderella saw a very old lady with a long ebony stick standing beside her. "Did nobody ever tell you that you had a fairy godmother?" asked the lady.

"When I was a tiny child somone did," said Cinderella, "but I thought you had forgotten me."

"No, indeed," declared the fairy. "I never forget, but I choose my own time to show that I remember. Now tell me, child, would you like to go to the Prince's ball?"

"Oh," cried Cinderella, "I should like it more than anything!"

"Very well then, run out into the garden and bring me the biggest pumpkin you can find." Puzzled, Cinderella obeyed.

"Now," said the fairy, "go to the pantry and see if there are any mice." Cinderella went and found that there were seven mice in the pantry, six small and one large.

"Very good," said the fairy. "Now, check behind the garden wall and you will find six green lizards." Once more Cinderella did as she was told.

"Now," said the fairy, "shut your eyes while I count to seven." Cinderella did as she was told. As the fairy godmother counted, Cinderella heard some strange noises: First, she heard the tapping of the long ebony wand and then footsteps and the clattering of hoofs. When Cinderella finally opened her eyes, she found a magnificent gold coach drawn by six white horses, driven by a coachman and attended by six footmen in liveries of green and gold.

Cinderella glanced down at her shabby dress and at the same moment, she felt the touch of the wand on her shoulders. The faded cotton changed into silver cloth and her shoes turned into glass slippers.

"Enjoy yourself," said the fairy godmother, "but remember, you must be home by midnight. For at the stroke of twelve, your coach will become a pumpkin, your footmen will become lizards, and your dress will change back into striped cotton." Without waiting to be thanked, the lady vanished. Cinderella jumped joyfully into the coach and set off for the ball.

The Prince was dancing a minuet with the elder of the stepsisters, when suddenly the music stopped and all the dancers turned toward the entrance of the ballroom. Cinderella had arrived and her beauty, together with her dazzling gown, had created such a stir that for a moment the fiddlers could not fiddle and the dancers could not dance. The Prince immediately dropped the stepsister's hand and went to greet the mysterious guest. For the rest of the evening, the Prince danced with no one except the beautiful stranger. The stepsisters would have been very angry, but Cinderella asked that

Cinderella

they should be presented to her and she talked with them so charmingly that their frowns soon turned to smiles.

The hours flew by swiftly. While Cinderella was sitting at supper, the clock struck quarter to twelve. Startled, Cinderella rose and said that, alas, she must now leave. The guests rose from the table and crowded in the hall to see her go. The Prince himself helped her into her coach, while the stepsisters stood on the marble staircase, waving their handkerchiefs.

When Cinderella arrived back in her kitchen, the fairy godmother was waiting for her. The moment her pretty glass slippers touched the floor, they vanished, and her silver gown turned into her old dress.

"Good child," said the fairy. "There is another dance tomorrow night and you shall be there. But remember, you must leave the palace when the clock strikes twelve, or you know what will happen." With these words, the fairy godmother vanished, and moments later the family coach rolled up to the door.

While Cinderella was helping them to undress, the stepsisters told her all about the ball. "Such a lovely supper!" cried the younger.

"And the Prince," shrieked the elder, "Not only is he handsome but gentle and so kind!"

"And the mysterious Princess!" they cried together. "I am sure she will be our Queen someday, and then we shall be invited to court, for I'm sure she took a great liking to us."

"What was she like?" asked Cinderella.

"She dances like a fairy," answered the younger stepsister. "And she has such tiny feet."

"And her hair," added the elder, "is the most wonderful color."

"Is it like mine?" asked Cinderella.

"Like *yours*? Why I never heard of such a thing! Why everyone knows that your hair is the color of carrots!"

"Hurry up, Cinderella," screamed the stepsisters. "You must put our hair in curlers at once. We want to look our best for tomorrow's ball."

"I wish I could go," sighed Cinderella.

"*You!*" laughed the stepsisters. "I never heard of such a thing!"

The next evening, no sooner had the mean stepsisters departed than the pumpkin coach arrived. This time Cinderella's gown changed into golden cloth, but she found the same pair of little glass slippers on her feet.

The Prince was waiting for Cinderella at the foot of the marble staircase. This time instead of ceasing to play when she entered the ballroom, the fiddlers struck up their merriest tune, and the Prince and Cinderella started the ball. The minutes flew even more quickly than the night before, and in the delightful company of the Prince, Cinderella forgot all about her fairy godmother's warning. The Prince led Cinderella out to the balcony so that she might admire the palace gardens. Then from the distant belfry of the cathedral, the great bronze bell began to toll midnight.

Cinderella gave a cry of alarm, gathered up her golden gown, and fled. The Prince ran after her, but when he reached the gateway of the palace, Cinderella had vanished from sight. The Prince asked the sentinels on guard if they had seen a princess in a golden gown drive away in a golden coach. They shook their heads. Neither of them thought to mention the little ragged girl who had sped up the road a minute before.

Puzzled, the Prince returned to the balcony to see if, by any chance, he could catch a gleam of the golden coach on the road far below. But, no such coach was to be seen, and so, sadly, the Prince turned away. As he did, he saw a gleam of silver at his feet. It was one of the glass slippers. The Prince had it placed carefully in a silver box in the hope that the owner might claim it. But weeks passed and no owner stepped forward. So the Prince sent his herald far and wide to proclaim that whoever could fit her foot into the pretty little shoe should be his bride.

Great was the excitement of all the unmarried ladies in the kingdom. Wherever the herald stopped, hundreds of ladies came running, all eager to see if they could squeeze their feet into the shoe. Among the ladies who tried were the mean stepsisters. Every-

body smiled when each one in turn kicked off her slipper and thrust forth her large, clumsy foot.

When they were finished trying, a timid voice asked, "May I try?" and Cinderella came forward.

"Go away, you absurd creature!" screamed the two stepsisters. "Go home at once and scrub the kitchen floor."

"Pardon me, ladies," said the herald, "but it is the wish of His Royal Highness that no one should be refused permission to try on the glass slipper."

With the herald was a man whose face was completely hidden in a dark cloak. This man now stepped forward, took the glass slipper out of the silver box, and arranged a purple cushion at Cinderella's feet.

Cinderella stretched forth her foot. The herald slipped the glass slipper on as easily as if it had been five sizes too large. At the same moment, the faded cotton dress changed into a gown of silver and gold.

The herald's companion threw back his hood and there stood the Prince. The crowd raised joyful cheers of "Long live our Prince! Long live our Princess!"

"Cinderella," squeaked the two stepsisters, "can you ever forgive us?"

"Who are these ladies, dear Princess?" asked the Prince as he took Cinderella by the hand.

"My stepsisters," said Cinderella.

"Then I suppose we must ask them to our wedding," remarked the Prince.

"Of course we must!" answered Cinderella stepping into his coach. Then she and the Prince set off for the palace, leaving the two stepsisters behind.

The original version of this story was first published in 1697. The illustrations are by Millicent Sowerby and were first published in 1915.

Rapunzel

THERE was once a man and a woman who wished very much to have a child. Near their cottage was a beautiful garden that belonged to a Witch. One day the wife looked over the garden wall and saw a bed full of the finest lettuce, and she so longed to eat them that she gave her husband no peace till he brought her one. She made a salad and ate it with great enjoyment.

In a few days, she began to long for more lettuce, and she again made her husband climb over the wall to fetch her some. He had no sooner seized a handful than he saw the Witch standing beside him.

"How dare you come into my garden?" she exclaimed fiercely. "You have stolen my lettuces, and now you must pay for them. If you have a child, you will give it to me or else you will be sorry." The husband, in great fear, gave his promise.

Soon after, a little daughter was born, and the Witch came and took her away. She named her Rapunzel and put her in a high tower in the forest. This tower had no stairs and no door and only one small window. When the Witch visited Rapunzel, she stood beneath the window, and cried:

"Rapunzel, let down your golden hair
That I may climb it like a stair."

Rapunzel had the most beautiful long hair, and when she heard the voice of the Witch, she let it hang over the windowsill right down to the ground, so that the Witch could draw herself up as if it had been a ladder.

When Rapunzel had grown into a beautiful maiden, it happened one day that the King's son was passing the tower and heard her singing. Her voice was so sweet that he longed to see her. The next day he came again to listen and the next. Then he heard the Witch call to Rapunzel beneath the window and saw her climb up by the maiden's long hair. The following night, when it was dark, he placed himself beneath the window and said:

"Rapunzel, let down your golden hair
That I may climb it like a stair."

Immediately the hair fell down, and he quickly climbed up and entered the tower.

Rapunzel was dreadfully frightened when she saw the Prince, but she soon lost all fear. After a time, he asked her if she would marry him, and she consented.

"I will bring you a strong silk cord," said the Prince, "so you can weave a ladder by which you will be able to descend from the tower. Then I will carry you to my father's castle, and we will be married."

Now the Witch had watched over Rapunzel very carefully, and she soon found out about the Prince's visits. She was very angry, and seized poor Rapunzel's golden hair and cut it off. Then she dragged her to a lonely place in the depths of the forest and left her there.

At sunset the Prince came to the tower, and cried:

"Rapunzel, let down your golden hair
That I may climb it like a stair."

The Witch let the hair down, and the Prince climbed up to the window. What was his horror to see, instead of Rapunzel, a hideous old Witch!

"Ah!" she cried, with a sneer, "you have come to carry off your bride! Rapunzel has gone away, and you will never see her again."

On hearing this, the Prince was so overcome with grief that he sprang out of the window and fell among the thorn-trees beneath. The thorns stuck into his eyes and blinded him, and he wandered away into the wood, lamenting and calling the name of his lost bride.

For a whole year he wandered, until at last he came to the lonely place where the Witch had left Rapunzel. He heard her singing and followed the sound until, on coming near, he was clasped in her arms. When she saw that he was blind she began to weep, and two of her tears fell on his eyes and healed them. Then Rapunzel and the Prince traveled back to his father's kingdom, and soon afterwards they were married, and lived in peace and happiness for the rest of their lives.

The original version of this story was first published in 1812. The illustrations are by an anonymous artist and were first published in 1909.

Aladdin and his Magic Lamp

THERE once lived a widow who had a son named Aladdin. One day, a magician stopped to watch Aladdin and his friends at play. He called Aladdin and asked him if he were not the son of Mustapha the tailor? Aladdin replied that he was but that his father had been dead for some years. At this news, the magician began to weep.

"Alas, my poor brother!" he sobbed. Then he said, "Dear nephew, greet your mother for me, give her this purseful of money, and tell her that I will visit tomorrow."

When Aladdin told his mother what had happened, she was puzzled because she knew that her husband had had no brothers. But the coins in the purse were good, so she prepared for the visit. Toward dusk the magician arrived.

"Tomorrow," he declared to Aladdin, "you must come with me to the tailor's, so that you may be clothed as befits a merchant's son."

After taking Aladdin shopping, the magician led him out into the open country.

"Now," he said, "gather some sticks and we'll light a fire."

When Aladdin had made a pile of sticks the magician muttered some strange words and set fire to the wood. A dark pillar of smoke rose from the fire. The earth trembled and cracked. Then a stone with a brass ring in the center appeared at the feet of the astonished boy.

"Aladdin," said the magician, "beneath that stone lies buried a treasure which only you can free. Take hold of that ring, utter the names of your father and your grandfather, and lift the stone."

Aladdin did as he was told. He then saw a steep flight of steps, at the foot of which was a narrow door.

"Listen, my nephew," said the magician. "Beyond that door you will find three halls brimming with gold. Beyond the third hall you will reach a garden. Beyond the garden is a marble terrace. On the terrace, there is a lamp. Bring it to me. If you value your life, touch nothing. But on your way back, you may pluck some of the fruit in the garden. Here is a ring which will protect you from danger. Now, be gone."

Everything happened exactly as the magician had foretold. On his way back, with the lamp carefully tucked into his jacket, Aladdin remembered that he might pluck some of the fruit in the garden. It was very odd-looking fruit, very hard and cold. Still, these balls of colored glass were pretty. So he stuffed his pockets with them.

"Pray, uncle!" the boy called, as he struggled up the steps with his heavy burden. "Help me up!"

The magician, who had never intended Aladdin to come out of the underground cave at all, saw that his wicked plan was not succeeding.

"Give me the lamp first," said the magician.

"Indeed, uncle, I cannot. But as soon as I am up, I will gladly give it to you."

The magician fell into a fearful rage. He uttered some more strange words. The heavy stone moved back into place. Then, having given up hope of getting the lamp, the magician vanished.

Aladdin was now in a sad plight. He called out, but there was no reply. He sat wringing his hands in despair and happened to rub the ring which the magician had given him. Immediately a genie stood before him, saying, "I am the Genie of the Ring! Command, and I shall obey."

When Aladdin had recovered from his terror, he replied, "Whoever thou art, set me free!"

A moment later, he found himself in the open air. Overjoyed, Aladdin hurried home.

The next morning when Aladdin woke up and asked for something to eat, his mother answered, "Alas, my son, we have nothing."

"Mother," said Aladdin, "I will take that old lamp and sell it."

Aladdin's mother fetched the lamp. It looked very grimy and it occurred to her that her son might get more money for it if it were cleaner. No sooner had she started rubbing than the genie stood before her, saying, "I am the Genie of the Lamp. Command, and I shall obey."

The poor woman was so terrified that she fainted. But Aladdin seized the lamp and said to the genie, "I am hungry. Bring me some food."

An instant later the genie set down a silver tray laden with silver dishes of food. Then the genie vanished.

The widow and her son lived very comfortably for several days upon the fare provided by the Genie of the Lamp. When they wanted money, all that Aladdin had to do was to sell one of the silver dishes. And when their food ran out, it was a simple matter to rub the lamp and call for more.

By frequenting the shops of silversmiths and jewelers, Aladdin soon learned a great deal about precious stones. It was not long before Aladdin realized the value of the fruit which he had gathered in the magic garden. Each piece of fruit, it turned out, was really a precious gem.

One fine day, Aladdin heard a royal herald proclaiming that everyone must go indoors while the Emperor's daughter went by. Aladdin was immediately seized with an overwhelming desire to behold the Princess. So he hid himself. When the Princess passed by, Aladdin saw that she was as beautiful as a bird of paradise. He could not stop thinking of her.

"What ails you, my son?" asked the widow.

"I love the Princess Badroulboudour," replied Aladdin. "And, as I cannot possibly live without her, I have decided to ask her

hand in marriage. Good mother, you must be my messenger to the Emperor."

"My son," she exclaimed, "I should never dare to open my mouth in the presence of the Emperor! At the very sight of him I should fall down in terror. You know that nobody dares approach the Emperor without offering him a gift. What have we that we could offer so great a king?"

"We have those fruits from the magic garden," returned Aladdin. "You shall see that the Emperor will not scorn our gift!"

When the widow saw the beauty of the jewels flashing and glittering, she felt less frightened. The next morning she went to the palace. The Grand Vizier approached her. With a wave of his hand, he led her to the Emperor himself. When she found herself face-to-face with the monarch, Aladdin's mother bowed to the ground.

"Rise, good woman," said the Emperor. "Tell me, why have you come?"

"O King of Kings," returned Aladdin's mother, "I beg that thine ears alone may hear what I have to say."

The Emperor commanded everyone but the Grand Vizier to withdraw and then bade the widow to tell her story. This she did and in conclusion she lay the precious stones at the Emperor's feet and requested the hand of the Princess on behalf of her son.

The Emperor was amazed at the beauty of the jewels. For a few minutes he remained silent. Then he exclaimed to the Grand Vizier, "Look, and wonder! Is not such a gift worthy of the Princess, my daughter?" The Grand Vizier could not deny the beauty of the jewels, but he was by no means pleased, for he had hoped that his own son might marry the Princess. So he answered, "But your Majesty knows nothing of the giver. Grant me, O King, a space of three months and my son shall bring yet a nobler gift."

So the Emperor said to Aladdin's mother, "I do not refuse your request. But neither can I grant it. Come again in three months."

Full of joy, the widow hurried home.

It chanced one evening that Aladdin's mother went to the marketplace. There, she was surprised to find silk banners and green garlands hanging from the houses.

Aladdin's mother asked a merchant what was the cause of the celebration.

"Why," he exclaimed in surprise, "had you not heard that tonight the son of the Grand Vizier is to be married to the Princess Badroulboudour?"

The poor woman hurried home and told Aladdin this startling news. Aladdin seized the lamp and rubbed. Instantly the genie stood there, saying, "I am the Genie of the Lamp. Command, and I shall obey."

"Genie," said Aladdin, "the Princess Badroulboudour and the son of the Grand Vizier are to be married tonight. As soon as the bride and bridegroom are alone, bring them both hither!"

"I hear and obey!" exclaimed the genie.

The genie flew to the palace and took up the bride and bridegroom. He carried them swiftly through the air to the house of Aladdin's mother, where he immediately locked the bridegroom in a cupboard. Meanwhile, Aladdin fell on one knee before the Princess, saying humbly, "Oh, beautiful Princess, have no fear! No one shall harm you! The Emperor had promised you to me and it was in order to make him keep his vow that I carried you off. Sleep well, O Princess! When morning comes, you shall be safely restored to the palace of your father! But you must tell no one what has happened."

The next morning, the genie transported the bride and the bridegroom back to the palace. The bridegroom flung himself at the Emperor's feet and sought permission to give up his claim to the hand of the Princess. The Emperor was surprised, but seeing that both the bride and bridegroom seemed determined to stop the wedding, he granted the request and the festivities came suddenly to an end.

As soon as the three months passed, Aladdin again sent his

mother to the royal chamber. When the Emperor saw the widow, he guessed what her errand must be.

"Good woman," said the Emperor, "I am ready to keep my word. But your son must first send me forty golden trays laden with jewels."

Now, the Emperor, who did not wish to give his only daughter in marriage to a stranger, imagined that he had set Aladdin an impossible task. Aladdin's mother thought the same but not Aladdin. Once again, he summoned the Genie of the Lamp.

When the Emperor saw how generously Aladdin had fulfilled his commands, all his doubts disappeared. He said to Aladdin's mother, "Tell your son to come hither, that his marriage with my daughter may be celebrated without delay."

When Aladdin heard this joyful news, he summoned the Genie of the Lamp yet again.

"Genie," said Aladdin, "bring me the most gorgeous garment ever worn by a King. Bring me a steed more beautiful than any other. I shall need forty servants, richly clad, to attend me."

When the Emperor beheld his son-in-law, he gave orders that the wedding festivities should begin at once. But Aladdin answered, "O King of Kings, let us wait until I have built a palace fit to be inhabited by the beautiful Princess Badroulboudour. Is there any space near your Majesty's own palace upon which I may be permitted to build?"

"Build wherever you wish!" returned the Emperor.

So Aladdin summoned the faithful genie. He ordered that a palace of colored marble and rare stone be erected. Great was the astonishment of the Emperor when he beheld this dazzling sight.

For several years, Aladdin and the Princess lived very happily in their splendid palace. Aladdin never rode forth without having a servant on either side who scattered gold among the people. So he soon became exceedingly popular, and the fame of his kindheartedness spread all over the world.

When the magician learned of Aladdin's marriage with the Princess Badroulboudour, he became terribly angry and mounted his magic horse. Aladdin happened to be out hunting and, of course, he had not taken the lamp with him. When the magician learned this, he had an idea. He went straight to Aladdin's palace. As he drew near he began to shout, "New lamps for old, new lamps for old."

The Princess heard this and she remembered her husband's tarnished old lamp. So she bade one of the servants fetch it and offer it to the peddler in exchange for a new one. When the magician saw the lamp, he snatched it hurriedly and gave the servant a new one. Then the magician rubbed the lamp. When the genie appeared, he said, "I command you to transport Aladdin's palace back to my world!"

The next morning the Emperor arose and went to the window to peek at Aladdin's palace. But the palace was not to be seen! He quickly summoned the Grand Vizier.

"Your Majesty," returned the Grand Vizier, "I have always expected it to vanish some day, as the works of magicians are wont to vanish!"

At the words of the Grand Vizier the Emperor became terribly angry.

"Go," he said, "await the villain. When he returns, bring him hither that he may be punished!"

Delighted, the Grand Vizier hurried away.

But when the people saw their beloved Aladdin being led through the streets of the city they made such an uproar that the Emperor made the executioner cover his sword and announced that Aladdin had been pardoned.

The first thing that Aladdin did when he found himself face-to-face with the Emperor was to demand why he had been seized.

"Wretch," replied the Emperor, "where is your palace? Where is my daughter?"

Aladdin looked out of the window and saw, to his dismay, that the palace had vanished.

To the Emperor he said, "O King of Kings, I know not by what means my palace has been removed, neither do I know where it may be! Grant me but forty days grace. If at the end of that time I have not discovered the whereabouts of the Princess, I will submit to whatever fate you decide"

"So be it," replied the Emperor, "but if you fail to find my daughter, do not hope to escape the consequences of my wrath!"

For three days, Aladdin wandered far and wide, but he found no trace of the palace or the Princess. At the end of the third day, he sat weeping and wringing his hands. He chanced to rub the magic ring and an instant later, the genie stood before him, saying, "I am the Genie of the Ring. Command, and I shall obey!"

"Genie," cried Aladdin, "I command you to return my palace to me."

Aladdin and his Magic Lamp

"To obey is not in my power," returned the genie. "You must ask my brother, the Genie of the Lamp."

"Well, then," said Aladdin, "wherever my palace may now be, take me there and set me down below the window of the Princess Badroulboudour."

A moment later, Aladdin found himself standing outside his castle.

At that very moment, the Princess looked out her window. Great was her astonishment when she beheld Aladdin standing beneath it! She summoned Aladdin to enter the palace.

After they had shed many tears of joy at their reunion, Aladdin said, "I beg you, most beautiful Princess, tell me what has happened to the lamp?"

The Princess then told him what had happened. She added that the magician came to see her every day and that in the innermost folds of the magician's tunic she had seen the lamp.

"Beautiful Princess," exclaimed Aladdin, "the magician is a false scoundrel, but I will show you a way by which we may get the better of him! Take this powder and dissolve it in a goblet of wine. When the magician comes to visit you tonight, invite him to drink with you. He will not refuse an honor so great."

Aladdin then left and hid just outside the palace.

That evening, the magician arrived at the usual hour. No sooner was he seated than the Princess offered him a goblet of wine. Delighted, the magician drank every drop. A moment later he fell backward, senseless.

At a signal from the Princess, Aladdin slipped into the palace and recovered the lamp.

The next morning the Emperor was looking sadly out of his palace window, when suddenly he began to rub his eyes. Aladdin's palace stood again in all its splendor.

As the Emperor had no sons, Aladdin in due course succeeded him upon the throne and ruled long and happily with his Empress, the beautiful Princess Badroulboudour.

The original version of this story was first published in 1704. The illustrations are by Albert E. Jackson and were first published in 1920.

Hansel and Gretel

ONCE upon a time, there lived a woodcutter who had a son named Hansel and a daughter called Gretel. Their mother had died when they were quite young, and after a time, their father married a second wife who was not at all kind to her stepchildren. Although he worked very hard, the woodcutter could not earn enough to feed the whole family, and there were often empty platters on the table.

One night, when the woodcutter thought his children were asleep, he told his wife that he was worried they would soon have no food to eat.

"There is only one thing to be done," said the cruel woman. "Early tomorrow, we will take the children into the very heart of the forest and leave them."

"I cannot leave them in the forest to be eaten by wild beasts," cried the woodcutter.

"There is nothing else to be done," answered his wife. Then she rolled over and went to sleep.

When Hansel and Gretel heard what their stepmother said, Gretel began to weep.

"Hush," whispered Hansel, "don't be afraid. I have a plan."

As soon as the woodcutter and his wife were asleep, Hansel tiptoed out into the moonlight. The grass outside was sprinkled with white pebbles that shone like drops of silver. Hansel filled his pockets with these pebbles and then went softly back to his room.

Early the next morning, the stepmother woke the children. "Up, you lazy creatures!" she said. "Your father is going into the forest to chop wood and we are all going with him."

As they walked along, Hansel secretly dropped the pebbles along the path. When they reached the heart of the forest, the woodcutter told the children to gather some twigs and make a fire. When the fire was lit, the stepmother said, "Now, you two children can sit by the flame and eat your dinner. Your father is going to cut wood nearby, and I am going to help him."

Hansel and Gretel were frightened, but the sound of their father's axe comforted them, for they knew that while they heard it he could not be far away. The children soon became drowsy and at last they fell asleep. When they woke, the forest was dark, but still they heard the chop, chop, chop of their father's axe. They scrambled to their feet and ran toward the sound, but all they found was a broken branch tied to a tree. The wind made the branch swing to and fro, and, as the stepmother had planned, it sounded just like the blows of an axe.

"Don't worry," said Hansel, "the moon is rising. Look, there are the pebbles. We'll find our way home." They set off hand-in-hand and by daybreak they arrived at the woodcutter's hut. The stepmother was quite dismayed to see them, but their father rejoiced.

After a few days, food began to run low and the woodcutter's wife said, "Those children of yours eat the shelf bare. There is only one thing to be done."

"I will not do it," said the woodcutter.

"We will do it tomorrow morning," said the wicked stepmother. Then she rolled over and went to sleep.

The children heard what she said, but this time they were not worried. But when Hansel tried to go outside to gather some pebbles, he found that the door had been locked.

"Don't be afraid," he said. "I will think of another plan."

At dawn the next day, the stepmother woke them and gave them a piece of bread. Hansel took the bread, broke it into small crumbs, and put the crumbs in his pocket. Then, again, he secretly dropped the crumbs along the way.

When they reached the very depths of the forest, they were told to gather sticks as before. When the fire was lit, the stepmother said, "Sit here till we come back for you. We shall not be gone long."

When the moon began to rise, the children started to look for the crumbs, but not a single crumb could they find. The birds had eaten every one.

Just as they were beginning to lose heart, the children came upon a little house. They had never seen a house quite like it before. The walls were made of cake, the windows of candy, and the roof of gingerbread,

"What a nice house!" cried Gretel.

"I'm going to find out what such a house tastes like!" said Hansel, as he tiptoed up and broke off a piece of the roof. They were feasting joyously when the door of the house opened and a very old woman came tottering out. The children were so frightened that they dropped their food on the ground, but the old woman did not seem at all cross.

"Come closer, children," she said. "My eyes are not the best, but you are both welcome." She passed her hands over their faces and muttered to herself, "They are thin now, far too thin, but we can soon fix that." Then she said, aloud, "Come in, my dears, come in. I am very fond of children."

Hansel and Gretel had never met anyone so kind. They followed her into the house where they found a table spread for supper.

"You shall have pancakes for supper," promised their new friend.

Never in their wildest dreams had Hansel and Gretel imagined that there could be such good things to eat. And for the first time in a long while, the two children went to bed happy.

Now this old woman who seemed so kind was really a witch and when she said that she was fond of children, she meant that she was fond of them for breakfast and dinner. Her gingerbread house was simply a trap.

When Hansel opened his eyes the next morning, he found himself in a wicker cage. Gretel was still asleep in her bed. Just as Hansel was going to call to her to set him free, the old witch came hobbling in.

"Wake up, child," said the old witch. "You must go to the well and draw some water, for I want to cook something nice for your brother's breakfast."

"Am I not to have any breakfast?" asked Gretel.

"Not as big a breakfast as his," returned the witch. "I want to make him nice and fat, so that he'll taste good when I eat him for supper."

Poor Gretel burst into tears at the thought of her brother being this witch's supper. And Hansel himself felt very much like crying. For four long weeks the witch kept Hansel in the wicker cage, feeding him all sorts of delicious food. Every morning, she would say, "Boy, stretch out your finger. I want to feel if you're getting fat." And every morning, Hansel would stretch out a piece of bone he had found in the cage. The witch was so blind, she could not see that it wasn't his finger, but she wondered why he was taking so long to fatten up.

At last she became impatient. "Gretel," she said one morning, "I will wait no longer. You must help me heat the oven."

Shedding bitter tears, Gretel lit the fire under the oven. Soon it was crackling and blazing.

"I think it must be hot enough now," said the witch. "Put your head in and tell me."

Gretel stuck her head in, and though it was really quite warm, she said, "It is still cold. You could never cook anything in such an oven."

"Add more logs to the fire," commanded the witch.

The logs spurted and flamed as the oven grew fearfully hot. "Put your head in again," ordered the witch.

"It's not hot yet," declared Gretel.

"You are tricking me!" cried the witch.

"See for yourself," answered Gretel.

Hansel and Gretel

When the witch opened the oven door, Gretel quickly pushed her and she fell head-over-heels into the oven. Gretel shut the oven door and locked it. Then inside the oven there was a big bang.

Meanwhile, Gretel ran to the cage and set Hansel free. They kissed each other and danced around the room.

Just then, there was another bang and the oven door swung open. Out popped a huge gingerbread cookie in the form of the old woman.

"I should not like to eat any of that gingerbread," said Hansel.

"No," agreed Gretel, "but let's take some of the walls and windows."

They began to explore the house and found that all the drawers and cupboards were filled with gold coins. The children filled their pockets and decided to try to find their way home.

They walked all day through the forest. Toward sunset, they saw the smoke rising from the chimney of the woodcutter's hut. Tired as they were, they began to run toward the little house, and as they ran the coins tumbled out on the grass.

The woodcutter was standing very sadly by the door of his hut. The cruel stepmother had died and he was now quite alone. When he saw his children running toward him, he could hardly believe his eyes. They were all so happy to be together again that it was some time before they thought about gathering up all the coins. But when they did, they discovered that there was more than enough to keep them comfortable for the rest of their lives.

The original version of this story was first published in 1812. The illustrations in this story are by Charles Robinson, and were first published in 1911.